Posy Bates and the Bag Lady

'Old lady, looks dumpy but isn't, because she's got lots of layers of old clothes. Frizzy grey hair and green and white – no, grey – striped woolly hat. Piece of string tied round middle. Tatty mitts with dirty fingers and black fingernails poking out.' Underneath the picture she wrote, 'If seen, tell Posy Bates immediately. DO NOT (underlined several times) tell the police.'

Also by Helen Cresswell

Meet Posy Bates
Posy Bates, Again!

Posy Bates and the Bag Lady

HELEN CRESSWELL
Illustrated by Kate Aldous

RED FOX

A Red Fox Book

Published by Random House Children's Books
20 Vauxhall Bridge Road, London SW1V 2SA

A division of Random House UK Ltd
London Melbourne Sydney Auckland
Johannesburg and agencies throughout the world

First published by The Bodley Head Ltd 1993

Red Fox edition 1994

3 5 7 9 10 8 6 4 2

Printed and bound in Great Britain by
Cox & Wyman Ltd, Reading, Berkshire

RANDOM HOUSE UK Limited Reg. No. 954009

ISBN 0 09 916451 5

*For the children of Gilthwaites First
School who have created a Butterfly
Garden in the World's Biggest Pie Dish*

One

Posy Bates was playing hide-and-seek with the bag lady. It was no ordinary game, either.

'It's in dead earnest,' she thought. 'Life or death, practically.'

She knew for a fact that the bag lady had been reported to the police by Mary Pye's mother.

'As if it was a *crime*, being homeless!' Posy thought indignantly. 'Anyway, she won't be much longer.'

Soon the bag lady would have a roof over her head. Admittedly, it was the roof of an old hen-house, but none the worse for that. Posy meant to turn that hen-house into a palace – or thereabouts.

She had not yet broken the news to Daff, her mother, that a bag lady was coming to live in the garden.

'I'll wait till I've got it all furnished, with

pictures and little mats and bunches of flowers, and really like home.'

Daff was not really hard-hearted, even if she sometimes pretended to be. After all, she had allowed Buggins, who was a stray dog, to stay. So there was no reason why she should object to a stray bag lady.

'Pity that hen-house hasn't got a bathroom, though,' she told Buggins. 'She's dead mucky, that old bag lady.'

His tail stirred. He was watching her eagerly, waiting for her to jump out of bed. You could hardly expect him to know it was Saturday. For Posy, each day of the week had its own special colour, and Saturday was best of all, a glorious, blazing yellow. And on that day Posy would lie in bed for a while, savouring the lovely yellow hours that lay ahead, hatching her plans.

'Two main things to do today,' she told him. 'Finish the hen-house, and find the bag lady. Bet you'll be able to find her. Bet your nose can sniff people out like anything!'

She herself had searched fruitlessly for her the night before. She had searched till it was nearly dark, and got ticked off for coming home late.

'But I've only got an ordinary nose,' she told Buggins. 'Not like yours.'

She looked dubiously at his round, black button of a nose, and could not help feeling that if it were longer and sharper it would be better for sniffing with. On the other hand, the bag lady was rather smelly, she had to admit. You wouldn't have to have the world's sharpest nose to sniff her out.

'Come on!' she said. 'Breakfast!'

Daff looked up from cutting bread as Posy entered the kitchen.

'Oh, there you are! And what's all this I hear?'

'All what?' asked Posy, wondering what she could possibly have done wrong already, in the two minutes since she'd got up.

'Kicking Mary Pye, that's what! Leg's black and blue this morning, her mother says.'

'Good,' said Posy heartlessly. She did not usually go round kicking people, but Mary Pye had asked for it – going on and on about homeless people deserving to be, and her mother

3

ringing up the police about the bag lady.

'Good?' echoed Daff. 'That doesn't sound like "sorry" to me, Posy Bates!'

'It's not meant to,' said Posy. 'I'm not sorry.'

'Then you'd better be,' Daff told her. 'Sharp!'

'You can't be sorry if you're not sorry, and if you're not sorry you can't say you're sorry because it'd be a fib, and then you'd have to be sorry for telling a fib, and I bet that was the sentence with the most sorrys in it that's ever been said!' finished Posy triumphantly. As an afterthought she added, 'Mind you, I bet if I try I can do a sentence with even *more* sorrys, and make it a World Record. I could even be in *The Guinness Book of Records*!'

One of Posy's dearest wishes was to be in *The Guinness Book of Records*. She didn't know what for. She just wanted to be in there, alongside the only man in the world to have eaten a bicycle, the World Champion Onion Peeler and the Best Bubblegum Blower in the world.

She had toyed with the idea of breaking the record for the Biggest Collection of Spiders in the world, or eating the most milk chocolate, or having the most brilling ideas in a single day. She didn't much care what it was for (apart from eating the most worms, of course, or having the most wasp stings), as long as she was in there. Daff had more than once suggested that she might be in for the untidiest bedroom, but Posy Bates knew sarcasm when she heard it.

'If you can't say sorry without *being* sorry,' Daff said now, 'then you'd better get to work on feeling sorry, and quick. Because say it you will, Posy Bates. And what did you want to go kicking Mary Pye for, anyhow? First time I've known you kick anyone, I will say that.'

'I kicked her,' said Posy, 'because she said the homeless *deserved* to be, and that they were mucky and smelly.'

'Got that from her mother, I shouldn't wonder,' said Daff. 'Germ mad, that woman. Could eat your dinner out her dustbin.'

Posy giggled.

'She even washes Mary's pencil case! Her pencil case! I bet that could be in *The Guinness Book of Records*!'

'It's no use your changing the subject,' Daff told her. 'You go round there and say you're sorry, the minute you've had your breakfast, you hear?'

'Can't,' said Posy. 'Sorry.'

'Can't? You mean won't!'

'Both,' said Posy. 'Can't and won't. I've already told you why, Mum.'

'And it's not good enough,' Daff said. 'Get Fred out, will you, while I do your sausages.'

The Bates family always had sausages on

Saturdays – it was one of the things that made it a yellow day. But, as she trudged back upstairs, Posy could not help feeling that what had been a bright sunflower yellow was now already paling into a sort of lemony tinge.

'Oh gubbins!' said Posy Bates.

Fred was already wide awake in his cot, kicking his arms and legs as if he were trying to keep afloat, and staring up at the mobile Posy had made out of empty yoghurt pots. She had heard that mobiles gave babies an interest in their spare moments, and she was very keen that Fred should be interested during his every waking moment. She was training him up to be a genius.

'Morning, genius!' she said, because she had also heard that people tend to grow into what you expect them to be.

Fred moved his gaze from the mobile and gazed at her with his amazingly clear blue eyes. He smiled. Posy, delighted, smiled back. Fred, it seemed to her, was the one person in the world who was always whole-heartedly happy to see her. He seemed to think she was perfect.

She leaned over and picked him up, and he was deliciously soft and warm even if, as she had feared, damp. She laid him on the towel and started to pull off his sleep-suit.

'You're lucky,' she told him. 'Mum never gets mad at you. She is with me. Says I've got to go

round and say sorry to that revolting Mary Pye.
I'm not, though. I can't. I'm glad I kicked her –
I was glad when I did it, and I'm glad now.'

She could tell by the intentness of his gaze
that he was taking it all in.

'So if I say sorry, and I'm not, it'll be a fib,'
she went on. 'Not just a little one, but a great big
enormous one. In fact, a downright whopper!'

Fred's nappy was exceedingly soggy. She used
the very tips of her fingers to lift it off and drop
it in the bin.

'And you've got to tell the truth,' she continued. 'It's really important. You're too young to know, but you will soon, because one thing about geniuses is that they always tell the truth. It's one of the things that *makes* them geniuses.'

Fred gurgled and she leaned over and started to tickle him, to keep him gurgling. It was one of the best sounds she knew.

'Shan't see you much today,' she said. 'Got to do up the hen-house and find my bag lady. Better tell you something quick, now.'

Posy was always telling Fred things – it was part of the training. She decided to deliver a lecture as she put on a clean nappy.

'I know, I'll tell you about fibs, 'cos I don't expect you really knew what I was talking about just now. You're too young. A fib is when you say something that's not true – just little things. You know, like telling Mum you're going for a walk, when really you're going looking for a bag lady. That's what I'll do, later on. That's only a teeny fib, mind you, because I shall be going for a walk, but not just an ordinary walk.'

Fred curled and uncurled his toes.

'A really big fib's called a lie. Least, grown-ups call it that – we call it a whopper. Are you listening? The minute you're old enough, you must try really hard not to tell whoppers. Mum says lies will always find you out.'

'Posy! Posy!'

'Sausages ready,' Posy told him. 'Come on, smelly!' and she lifted him and carried him downstairs. She plonked him in his high chair and sat down. George, her father, had come in from the garden and had already started.

'Where's Pippa?'

Pippa was Posy's sister, and quite a lot older.

'Didn't want sausages. On a diet.'

'Oh yippee – can I have hers?'

'No, you can't. I've put them in your dad's box. He's off fishing.'

'What'll you do today, Posy?' he asked.

'Oh – just things.' Posy was deliberately vague, careful not to tell a fib.

'She's not doing anything till she's been and said she's sorry to Mary Pye,' Daff said.

'Oh, but Mum – '

'Don't "But Mum" me,' said Daff. 'You'll do it, and that's flat.'

'But I can't – I told you!'

'I'm getting sick of this, Posy,' said Daff, beginning to sound dangerous. 'If you can't say you're sorry, then you go straight up to your room and think about it till you can.'

Posy munched miserably, the delicious sausages gone to sawdust in her mouth. She said not another word. Daff and George were talking about the kitchen, and how it needed a coat of paint, but she did not really hear them. She usually had toast and marmalade after her sausages, but today she did not feel like it. She pushed back her chair and stood up.

'And where are you going?' enquired Daff.

'Up to my room, like you said.'

She was annoyed to find that tears were stinging her eyes. She blinked them away.

'I mean it, Posy!' Daff's voice came after her.

Posy knew that. She threw herself on her bed. She thought of the way she had meant to spend the day, busily making the hen-house a home from home. She thought about the bag lady. Perhaps by now the police had found her, and sent her to prison. She did not know whether you could be sent to prison for being a bag lady, but would not be surprised. Why else had Mrs Pye reported her to the police?

'I hate that Mary Pye!' she said out loud, and she felt again the choking fury she had felt last night, and knew that if Mary Pye was there now, she'd kick her again – even harder, this time. She'd probably black her eye, as well.

'What's that?' Pippa's head poked round the door. 'Talking to yourself? First sign of madness.'

'I *am* mad,' said Posy. 'Furious.'

'Oooh – wish I couldn't smell those sausages! Why? What's up?'

10

'It's Mum,' Posy said, and told her the story. She didn't tell the whole story – she didn't tell about doing up the hen-house, or the bag lady being her friend.

'Don't see the problem.' Pippa was examining her face, very closely, in the mirror. She was always doing that, as if she expected to find something she hadn't noticed before.

'I can't say I'm sorry when I'm not!'

'Tell you what *I* used to do,' said Pippa. 'Still do, sometimes. I'd say it, but I'd have my fingers crossed.'

Posy stared.

'What difference does that make?'

'Means you don't really mean it. They think you do, but you know you don't.'

11

Posy pondered. She was certainly keen to find a way out of the trap she was in, but could not for the life of her see that crossing fingers would help.

'Thanks,' she said. 'I'll think about it.'

'Suit yourself!' said Pippa, and was off, down to start her own sausageless day.

Posy had a good think about Pippa's suggestion, but couldn't see how it could possibly work.

'Just crossing fingers can't cancel out a whopper,' she thought. 'You cross fingers for *luck* – kind of magic – like twice round the garden shed, once round the sundial, clap your hands five times, shut your eyes and say the magic word!' (This was a charm Posy used herself, and as far as she could make out, it worked, usually.)

'I'll have to stop here forever, now,' she told Buggins bitterly. 'I'll be like Rapunzel in that tower. I might even grow my hair like hers – it'd give me an interest. I could measure it every day. It'd end up trailing all round the room and I'd have to watch out it didn't get tangled in the Hoover.'

She occupied herself for several minutes picturing herself with this phenomenal hair, which at any rate might get her into *The Guinness Book of Records*. Unfortunately, the book was kept on the shelves in the living room, so she couldn't check up to see if there *was* a record for the longest hair, and if there was, who held it, and what she had to beat.

All too soon, her thoughts went back to the bag lady and to her hen-house. She felt quite desperate.

'I s'pose one thing I could do is start making a picture, to hang up in there when it's all clean and tidy.'

She found some paper and paints and went to the bathroom for water.

'What'll I do a picture *of*? What'd she like?'

She really did not know the bag lady well enough to know what her taste in pictures was.

'Any case, if she wanders the wide world she won't know about pictures. Has a different home every night, I dare say. Can't have pictures under railway bridges, or on hedges.'

In the end, Posy decided on a picture of the bag lady herself.

'It'll make her feel important, having her portrait painted,' she thought. And she tried not to hear a small voice inside her head saying that then, if she never saw the bag lady again, the portrait would remind her of what she had looked like. Posy shut her eyes and summoned up the picture of that roly-poly figure cocooned in layers of cardies and coats, the flyaway hair under the knitted hat, the grimy fingers poking from the frayed mitts.

'Dear old bag lady!' thought Posy lovingly, and then remembered the magic bobbin the old lady had given her that first time, in the Victoria Centre. Her heart leapt. If anything could help her now, that bobbin could. She got up and took it from the biscuit tin on the window sill. To anyone else it might have looked like any empty cotton reel, but Posy knew differently. She held it in her hand, tight, and was about to shut her eyes when she saw Sam coming up the garden path.

She rapped on the window and he looked up. Posy opened the window.

'It's no good knocking on the door,' she told him. 'Mum won't let me play. I've to stop in my room till I say sorry, and I won't, not ever, so I'll be here forever and ever!'

'Sorry? What for?'

She told him. She told him about kicking Mary Pye and her leg being black and blue. She even told him about Pippa's idea about crossing fingers.

'But it won't work,' she said.

'No, it won't,' he agreed. 'But I know what will. 'S'easy!'

'You *do*?' She gazed at him. Sam Post had the answer? She could hardly believe it. He tended to leave all the brilling ideas to her – which was a good thing, because she had plenty.

''S'easy. Learned it long ago.'

'What? *What* then?'

'What you do is, you work out what you really mean to say. Like, "I'm sorry I kicked you, because now I'm stuck in my room, but what I really wish is that I'd kicked you ten times harder!" '

Posy stared at him in disbelief.

'I can't say that!'

'I haven't finished. Then, when you've worked it out, what you do is, you say the first part – the being sorry bit – out loud. And then you say the rest of it to yourself, inside your head!'

Posy gazed down at him as the idea sank in. If she said something like that, it'd be the absolute truth. What difference did it make if only part of it was said out loud? It was a good idea. It was, she reluctantly admitted to herself, an absolutely total, brilling idea.

'Well?' Sam demanded. 'Are you going to do it?'

She grinned.

'You're a genius – in patches! I'll do it! Thanks!'

She shut the window.

'Oh ace, oh total, oh absolutely brilling!' she sang. 'Oh Buggins – I'm free!'

She ran downstairs and into the kitchen.

'I'll do it! I'll say I'm sorry.'

Daff turned.

'That's a good girl. I knew you'd see sense. Doesn't cost anything to say sorry, Posy.'

'Does if it's a whopper!' said Posy – but not out loud, inside her head.

'I'm going now. Come on, Buggins!'

She raced off down the path, down the green tunnel of the lane, bursting, actually bursting now to say she was sorry. She laughed out loud at what she'd really be saying to that goody goody sneaking Mary Pye. As she went, she rehearsed it inside her head, so that when the time came she'd be word perfect.

She went through the Pyes' smartly-painted gate and up their trim garden path and rang their silly chiming bell.

Mrs Pye opened the door.

'Hello, Mrs Pye. I've come to say sorry to Mary – for kicking her.'

Mrs Pye gave Posy a look, then Buggins, as if she suspected them of leaving foot and paw marks on her path.

'I should think so, indeed!' She raised her voice. 'Mary!'

Next moment there she was, snooty, pasty-faced Mary Pye with her well-brushed hair and clean fingernails and shoes you could eat your dinner off. Posy looked at the leg she had kicked, the leg that was meant to be black and blue. There was the faintest possible, hardly notice-able, pale green bruise.

'Didn't kick her hard enough,' thought Posy. Then she took a deep breath, ready to say her piece.

'I'm sorry I kicked you,' (out loud) ' – but what I really wish is that I'd done it twice as hard, on *both* legs, and blacked both your piggy eyes!' (to herself)

She beamed. Mary Pye, puzzled, gazed blank-ly back at her.

''S'all right,' she said sullenly at last.

'Hurray!' yelled Posy Bates, and she turned

and ran. There was a missing bag lady to find, a
hen-house to decorate, a whole sunflower-yellow
Saturday ahead.

Two

'One job at a time.' Daff was always saying that. She said it to George, to Pippa and to Posy herself.

The trouble was that today Posy had *two* jobs, and she wanted to do them both first.

'Wish I could be in two places at once!'

This was an interesting thought. Would it mean splitting down the middle – a left-hand Posy in the hen-house, a right-hand Posy looking for the bag lady?

'Trouble is, I'd be hopping along on one leg, and only have one hand.'

'I've only got one pair of hands.' Daff was always saying that, too.

'I've only got half a pair of hands! That's what I'd be able to say.' She giggled – though it was not a giggling matter.

She had to find that bag lady, find her before

she left Little Paxton and set off again into the wide world, perhaps forever. On the other hand, the whole point of finding her was to offer her a home – a beautifully spick and span hen-house.

'If it's not finished, it won't look like home.'

Posy fished for a solution.

'The thing is, I'm the only one who can do the hen-house. No one else must even know about it, till it's done. But that bag lady – anywhere, she could be, and anyone could spot her.'

The bag lady had already been spotted in the village, not by Posy herself, but by quite a few people, including the disgustingly clean Mrs Pye. So . . .

'A reward!' Posy stopped dead at the suddenness and brilliance of her idea.

'That's what they do with missing persons. They put up a poster with a photo! And sometimes they give a reward – a hundred pounds, even a thousand!'

She started to run.

'Posy! Posy!'

Sam was hurrying after her, weighed down with Saturday morning shopping. She waited for him.

'I've said sorry,' she told him, 'and you should hear the part I said inside my head!'

She told him.

'It's a brilling idea,' she said generously. 'I'll

be able to do it for life, now. And listen, it's no use asking if I'm playing, 'cos I'm not. I'm busy. I'm up to my armpits. But if you want to earn two pounds, I can tell you how.'

'Two quid? How?'

She told him about the missing bag lady.

'I'm just going to make a poster,' she finished, 'but you've got a head start, because you'll be the first to look, *and* you know what she looks like. She gave you that goldfish, remember?'

'But why d'you want to find her?'

'Never you mind. It's a secret. Least, it is for now.'

'And you really are going to give two quid to whoever finds her?'

'Yes. I'd give a hundred, if I'd got it.'

'Oh well, might as well then, I s'pose.'

'Start now!'

'What, carrying this lot?'

'Give it here. I'll give it to your mum.'

Once Posy Bates had an idea, she liked to put it into action – even if it meant lugging two heavy bags, and being polite to Mrs Post.

Sam passed over the shopping and turned back towards the village. Then he stopped.

'Hey! What do I say to her if I do find her?'

'Don't say anything. Just run back, quick as you can, and tell me.'

He nodded and went on.

21

Posy had to let go of Buggins' lead, she couldn't possibly hold that and the bags.

'You can have a bit of a sniff round the hedge if you like,' she told him. She staggered on. Mrs Post saved all her shopping till Saturday.

'I'm a bag lady now,' she thought. 'A bag girl.'

And she started to imagine what it would really be like, if she were. For one thing, she could never get away from those bags. They'd hold every single thing she had in the world. They'd become as much a part of her as her own hands and feet.

'Everywhere, I'd have to take them,' she thought. 'Up hill, over dale, into Nottingham, over zebra crossings. Even when I went to the lav.'

Once she had exhausted the subject of the bags, Posy began to wonder how the bag lady decided where she would go each day. After all, if the whole wide world was the only home you had, it wouldn't make much difference.

'I think what I'd do is, I'd make a kind of game of it. When I woke up – under a hedge or a bridge somewhere – I'd decide, "Today I'm going to take one left turn and one right turn, alternately". Then, when that got boring, I'd turn left twice and right once.'

All the time, she supposed, and especially when it got towards evening, she would be looking for somewhere to sleep.

'And sometimes it rains, rains all day. Then what? And when I got wet, how would I get dry again?'

The more Posy thought about it, the gladder she was that she was a bag girl only for now.

She dumped the bags in the Posts' porch and banged on the knocker. Mrs Post answered. She stared.

'Whatever . . . ? That's my shopping! Where's Sam?'

Posy evaded the question.

'He won't be long. I said I'd just drop these off for him. 'Bye!'

Back in her room she set about making her poster.

'Was just going to paint her picture anyway,' she thought, staring at the paper she had put out ready for the portrait earlier on, and marvelling at her own foresight.

First she wrote the word 'MISSING' in red felt tip. Then, underneath, in even bigger letters, the word 'REWARD'. Underneath that she wrote '£2'. She sat back on her heels and gazed at it.

'Looks rather measly,' she thought. 'Look better with some noughts after it.'

On the other hand, she didn't *possess* any noughts. Nor, she now realized, did she have a photograph. Usually, in the middle of WANTED posters was a large photo.

'Or a photofit! That's it! I'll do one of those.'

Posy had seen plenty of photofits in newspapers and on television, and had often thought they all looked much the same. The men, in particular, always seemed to have the same glaring eyes and unbelievable hair. Even Daff had once remarked that if George was splashed all over everywhere as a photofit, she didn't suppose she'd recognize him.

'I'll do her head,' Posy decided. 'Then a description underneath.'

The head seemed a good idea, because of the woolly hat, and Posy did it in colour, because the hat was definitely green and white striped, and the hair grey and frowsty. The face wasn't easy, though. In fact, the more Posy thought about it, the more she realized that if she were to meet the bag lady in the street, hair cut and washed and wearing a smart new coat, she probably wouldn't recognize her.

'It's the layers of clothes and the bags.'

Posy could not remember seeing a full-length photofit, but she never minded departing from tradition if it seemed a good idea. It stood to reason, she thought, that the main thing anyone would notice about the bag lady was her roly-poly shape, her ragged mittens and bulging bags.

'I'll make the first full-length photofit in the history of the world,' she thought.

And so she did. She gave the bag lady only currants for eyes and a mere squiggle for a mouth and no nose at all. But she got the roly-poly shape right, the coat tied round the middle with string. And she made the hands somewhat larger than life, to show the mitts more clearly.

She added the bags and was satisfied. She held the picture at arm's length and squinted her eyes, the way Miss Perlethorpe did in art lessons.

'That's her, all right,' she decided.

She was quite pleased with the idea of drawing the bag lady rather than describing her. She couldn't help feeling that any description however tactfully phrased, would sound rude.

'Things about her being old and raggy,' she thought, 'and about her fingernails being dirty, and that.'

A description would have gone something like this:

'Old lady, looks dumpy but isn't, because she's got lots of layers of old clothes. Frizzy grey hair and green and white – no, grey – striped woolly hat. Piece of string tied round middle. Tatty mitts with dirty fingers and black fingernails poking out.'

Posy would not have liked the bag lady to come across such a description of herself. It would have hurt her feelings – it would hurt anyone's.

Underneath the picture she wrote, 'If seen, tell Posy Bates immediately. DO NOT (underlined several times) tell the police.'

She went downstairs.

'Anything from the shop, Mum?'

She had to go to the post office in any case,

to put up her poster. She might as well score some Brownie points at the same time.

Up at the shop, Mrs Parkins eyed the poster suspiciously.

'Is this a joke?'

'No,' replied Posy. 'It's deadly serious. Here's the twenty pence for putting it in the window. Shall I put it in?'

And so she did, among the notices advertising lawn mowers for sale, and asking for baby-sitters.

That done, she raced back home, free to get on with the transmogrification of the hen-house. So far, she had concentrated on the outside, with chopping down the weeds and nettles, and clearing a path to the front door. Now for the inside.

Luckily, half one whole side of the hen-house opened on a hinge. You could hardly expect the bag lady to climb through a hole meant for a hen. Posy pulled the door open and peered inside. It was dim in there, fusty and dusty.

'Doomy,' thought Posy Bates.

At the moment, it was more like the oven the witch pushed Hansel and Gretel into than the gingerbread house Posy saw in her mind's eye.

'Good sweep out, first,' she decided.

For the next hour or so she created a glorious dust. She had not known there was so much

dust in the world, and could not for the life of her think where it had come from.

'Perhaps it's everywhere, like air,' she thought, 'or perhaps hens make dust like they lay eggs.'

She only dimly remembered the time when there had been hens in there, clucking and crooning and laying their beautiful warm eggs. She could remember chasing them, too, when they ran round the garden, pecking at Daff's precious flowers. The bag lady was not much like a hen.

'And she certainly won't lay eggs!' Posy giggled, and hoped very much that she wouldn't run squawking round the garden, either.

Once the hen-house was swept, it certainly looked better than the bottom of a hedge, or a railway tunnel, but was still, to Posy's eye, dingy.

'What it needs is a lick of paint.'

She *heard* this idea, almost as a voice – Daff's voice, inside her head. As a matter of fact, she had heard Daff use those very words to George that morning.

'Always plenty of paint in the shed, anyway!'

She scrambled out of the hen-house, past Buggins who lay snoozing, and made for the shed.

'Posy! Posy!'

It was Sam.

'I've seen her, I've seen her!'

Posy let out a great whoop of joy and ran to meet him.

'Where? Where?'

He told her. Not without a lot of boasting first, though.

'I'm a Private Eye! I worked it out!'

It stood to sense, he said, that a bag lady wouldn't hang about in the middle of a village. There were too many people like Mrs Pye about.

'So I looked in the barns!'

'*Whose* barns?'

'Potters'! And there she was – cor, Posy, she isn't half mucky and smelly!'

'Twinkle twinkle little star
What you say is what you are,'

replied Posy calmly. She could hardly deny that the bag lady was both mucky and smelly.

'Did she see you?'

'Yes, she did. Didn't half give me a glare!'

'Probably knew you were a Private Eye,' Posy said. 'She doesn't glare at me.'

This was not strictly true. The bag lady had glared at her once or twice and always, truth be told, seemed on the *edge* of glaring.

Posy was moving fast all the time, in the direction of Potters' barn, Buggins and Sam at her heels. She stopped.

'Don't you come,' she told Sam. 'You'll frighten her off.'

'I found her!'

'And if she's still there, you'll get paid for it. Just go away, will you?'

'She won't be frit of me. Why should she?'

'Go away!' said Posy fiercely. The bag lady was hers.

'Gave me that goldfish, anyway.'

'Shut – up – and – go – away!'

He did go, then, shouting from a distance.

'Mind you don't catch fleas! Bet she's covered in 'em! Flea bag! Flea bag!'

Three

Posy was moving so fast in the opposite direction that Sam's words soon faded. But she wondered whether the bag lady *was* smothered in fleas? Posy's hobby of collecting insects had rather tailed off since the coming of Buggins. How easy would it be to catch a flea? They jumped very fast, from what she had heard.

'You'd better not get too close to her, old boy,' she told Buggins. By now, Daff had more or less accepted him, but might easily change her mind at first sight of a flea.

Now she was in the bare, stubbly field where the Potters' barn stood. She took a deep breath and marched steadily towards it. As she reached the ramshackle, half-open door, she heard a cracky voice, reciting. She stopped and listened.

'Icky this, icky that! Bother this and bother that!'

Posy did not really think that the bag lady might be a witch in disguise. The thought had crossed her mind, though – especially as the magic bobbin given to Posy on their first meeting did seem to work, rather.

'Icky this, icky that! Bother this, bother that!'

It didn't sound exactly like a spell, but it could be. On tiptoe now, Posy crept up and peered through a chink.

There, in the deep dimness of the barn, squatted the bag lady on a bale of hay. She had her bags by her and seemed to be picking through them. Posy had often wondered what she kept in there. Certainly not brush and comb and wash things. Spare layers of clothes for cold nights, perhaps, or newspapers for blankets? (One of the things Posy had learned at Brownies was that if you found yourself at night in freezing cold, you were to wrap yourself up in newspaper, like fish and chips.) Or maybe she had some books, or a torch and bars of chocolate?

'Bothersome muddle, bothersome muddle!'

Whatever the bag lady was looking for, she evidently could not find it. Back the things went into the bags, stuffed all anyhow.

Posy cleared her throat loudly and pushed the door. It creaked as it swung open and the bag lady looked up then, quick and sharp as a fox, eyes glinting in the gloom.

'It's me – Posy Bates!'

She knew then what Sam had meant about the glare. It went right into the marrow of her bones, right through her. If Posy had never met that bag lady before, she herself would probably have taken to her heels.

'Don't you remember me? At the Vicky Centre and at the fair?'

'Poky pry, poky pry, first him and now you!'

she spat the words out and Posy flinched.

'We're not spying, honest! We just wanted to warn you about the police, and – '

'Pleece? Pleece!!!!' The bag lady thrust the things into her bag faster than ever, then scrambled to her feet.

'No! No police! That's what I meant – '

'Where? Where?'

'Nowhere! Don't go! You're safe here.'

'Safe? What's safe? Hark hark, the dogs do bark!'

She was glaring at Buggins now, but he certainly wasn't listening. He was walking round the bag lady and her luggage and sniffing, in a heaven of rich smells, Posy supposed. The bag lady glared and glared and then, quite suddenly, sat down again. Her head nodded to and fro, she hugged herself and rocked from side to side.

'Icky gone, icky lost!' She was wailing now, to herself it seemed, Posy and Buggins forgotten. 'Gone gone gone!'

To her horror, Posy saw a fat tear squeeze from each of the bag lady's eyes and roll down her cheeks.

'Oh, what? Tell me – I'll find it for you! Don't cry!'

She wanted to pat her comfortingly on the arm, but dared not. It was bad enough to see any grown-up crying. When grown-ups cry, the

world goes suddenly unsafe and scary.

The bag lady's shoulders were shaking, she was sobbing in earnest now. Posy could not bear it. She went outside and stood, uncertain and miserable, in the wide, shaved field.

All her plans seemed suddenly silly and useless. She did not know exactly how she had been going to explain to the bag lady about the henhouse. She only knew that it was now impossible to say a single word about it. She had imagined the wrinkled face cracking in its first real smile for years. She could never have imagined it crumpled in such misery.

'What can she have lost? What?'

Surely not one of her tattered mitts? No one could weep so bitterly over a lost glove.

Posy Bates, for once in her life, simply did not know what to do. All she knew for certain was that now she had found the bag lady again, she didn't mean to lose her. And that meant that she could not go home and find some paint for the hen-house. Without its bag lady, the hen-house might as well stay as it was.

'Whatever she's lost, it could've been round here. Could've dropped it coming out the village.'

Posy hesitated. She hardly liked to lose sight of that barn, but guessed that the bag lady would be in no mood to move on just yet. She might stop there crying for hours.

'So what I could do, is go back to the village, the way she must've come, and keep my eyes skinned. If she did drop something, I might find it.'

The thought of finding the lost treasure (whatever it was), of handing it over to its owner and seeing that woebegone face light up with joy, was irresistible. She started back the way she had come – walking, this time.

It was not long before she began to feel dizzy. It was difficult enough straining your eyes left and right when you knew what you were looking for. Posy did not know. It could be anything.

'Hunt the thimble!' she thought, and fervently hoped that it was not. Buggins did a lot of snuffing, so she kept an eye on him, too.

'Could do with three eyes,' she muttered.

It was Buggins who found the article that was

the only possible lost property. By then they were back in the village, almost on the green. He snuffed and snuffed, and afterwards Posy wondered whether it was the whiff of the bag lady he had caught, or the scent of something else – a cat. She knew really, of course, that cats in photographs can't have scents, but all the same . . .

Posy stopped, stared, and picked it up. It was so entirely unexpected that her heart jumped.

It was a photo of a cat, mainly, a very large, fat, black and white cat. But it was being held in someone's arms, and that someone was wearing a frock with a pinny over, and was standing in what looked like a back yard, with a line of washing. That someone was not wearing a striped woolly hat. She had real hair that looked as if it might have been permed. That face was not wrinkled, but quite plump, and what was more, it was wearing the special kind of smile that people always wear for photos.

That someone was her bag lady.

Posy's heart did a somersault. She stared at the picture. It had given her one of the biggest shocks of her life. It was as if she had seen the frog in the fairy tale transmogrified into a prince before her very eyes.

She had rather thought of the bag lady as a creature of magic, even if not exactly straight out of a fairy tale. She had thought of her wandering the wide world not only homeless, but rootless, too. She had also thought of her as ageless, old as the hills. But in that photo she was definitely younger.

'So she wasn't *born* old,' Posy thought. And her main feeling was sadness, at the loss of a mystery. That magic wooden bobbin in her pocket seemed suddenly less magic.

'She's just a stray, really, like you,' she told Buggins. But she brightened somewhat at the thought that the bag lady would at least not be of interest to the RSPCA.

'And I don't suppose there's an RSPCBL,' she thought.

The cat in the picture did not look at all like a witch's cat, either. It was fat and smug and you could almost hear it purring.

Another thought struck her.

'Oh, she couldn't have been – she was never married and had children!'

She carefully scanned the blurred line of washing in the background for T-shirts and jeans. But it seemed to be towels and stockings, mostly.

'So she hasn't always been mucky. And wearing an apron!'

Her picture of the bag lady was turned all topsy-turvy now. She actually shut her eyes and tried to imagine her dusting and making beds and washing up. Then she would take off her pinny and sit down to a nice cup of tea and a chocolate digestive, cat purring in her lap. To her relief, she could not imagine it at all.

Being Posy Bates, she could not help casting round for a silver lining.

'But she might, once she's in the hen-house!'

Posy had not really looked beyond the magical

moment when she would triumphantly fling open the door of the hen-house and show the bag lady her marvellous nest. Perhaps she had not really wanted to. Daff was certainly not going to like the idea of a mucky bag lady squatting in her back garden. But a house-proud bag lady might be a different matter.

'Better hurry on back and give her this, anyhow.'

She was opposite the shop, with its sign
SANDWICHES TO ORDER
AND HOT PIES.

'Wait!' she told Buggins, and went in.

'Eating between meals, Posy Bates?' said Mrs Parkins, when Posy ordered the pie.

'It's for a friend, as a matter of fact.'

She ran all the way back to Potters' barn.

'Let her still be there, let her still be there!' the refrain ran in her head.

She was. The bag lady, eyes closed, sat where Posy had left her, motionless in the shadowy barn.

''S'me!' she whispered.

The bag lady's eyes flicked wide open in an instant. Posy had already decided, 'Pie first, then photo.'

'I've brought you this.'

The bag lady's mitted hand snatched the paper bag. There was not even a thank-you. Her

41

manners were certainly terrible. She gobbled the pie, cheeks bulging, and Posy watched, enchanted. Now that she was actually there again, large as life and twice as smelly, she was as magical as ever, quite unlike any other human being Posy had ever met before. The photo in her pocket paled and faded. It did not matter.

The bag lady wiped her mouth with her sleeve and looked intently at Posy, as if half expecting seconds, or a pudding to follow. She certainly did not say, 'Thank you, dear, that was delicious!' – nor did Posy expect her to.

For one mean moment Posy was tempted not to mention the photograph. She was, truth to tell, jealous of that cat. She felt that the bag lady was hers – had been from that first moment in Nottingham, in the Victoria Centre. *She* was the bag lady's family.

'I – I think I've found what you were looking for.'

Still the bag lady looked, saying not a word. Slowly, Posy withdrew the photo from her pocket and held it out.

It was snatched by a grimy hand so hungrily that it seemed in danger of following the pie straight into her mouth. She held it inches away from her small black eyes, and stared at it greedily, as if she were willing that cat to jump straight out of the picture and into her lap.

'Ah, there, icky puss,' she crooned. 'Pussy cat, pussy cat, where've you been?'

'I've been up to London to look at the Queen,' Posy supplied. 'It was on the green, actually. Buggins found it. Hey – that's good! "Pussy cat, pussy cat, where've you been? In Little Paxton, up on the green!" '

The bag lady was not even listening. She seemed to have forgotten Posy was there. Now she was making purring sounds – *purr, purr, purr*!

'Pity she couldn't have brought the cat with her, on her travels,' Posy thought. 'Dick Whittington did.'

She tried to picture it. The bag lady stomping on and on, up hill and down dale, and treading after her, a fat black and white cat, tail waving. It was an unlikely picture, but not an impossible one.

'Or what – what if the cat ran away, years ago, and that's why she's a bag lady? What if she's been roaming the wide world looking for it?'

The thought was almost unbearably sad. The old lady had stopped purring now. She took one final look at the cat, then thrust the photo deep into one of her pockets.

'Ding dong bell, pussy's in the well!' she said matter-of-factly.

She looked at Posy. The cat was forgotten,

and it was business as usual.

'Nice cat,' Posy lied. Actually, she had not particularly liked the look of the cat. It had struck her as fat and smug-looking, too pleased with itself by half. 'What's its name?'

The bag lady did not reply. She always seemed unwilling to talk at all. Her conversation had probably gone rusty during all those long, lonely marches. Posy realized that she was going to have to do most of the talking. Luckily, this was not a problem.

'I've been looking everywhere for you,' she said. She did not mention the poster, and the reward. 'I've got a surprise for you – a really mega one. Brilling.'

The bag lady did not seem to be listening. She was muttering under her breath and appeared to be counting on her fingers.

'The only thing is, it isn't quite ready yet, but it will be soon. So what I really wanted was to make sure you didn't go away till you've seen it.'

No reply.

'It's quite comfy here, though, isn't it? I mean, you'll be all right here till the surprise is ready? There's lots of straw.'

'*You* eat straw?' demanded the bag lady.

'No, of course – oh, I didn't mean that! I'll fetch you food, if you stop here.'

'Get the belly rumbles,' said the bag lady dolefully.

'You won't, I promise. I'll bring you bags and bags of stuff. Oh please say you'll stop!'

There was a particularly long silence. Posy held her breath.

'Stop a bitty,' said the bag lady at last.

'Oh hurray! Brilling! You stop here, and I'll be back later. I'll bring bags of food.'

'Don't drink dew, neither. Don't eat straw, and don't drink dew.'

'*And* drink!' cried Posy recklessly. 'Gallons of it! 'Bye!'

Four

Posy was off, running as fast as she could in a day miraculously brilliant yellow again. Buggins, catching her mood, jumped and yelped beside her. She was nearly home when she met Caroline Boot and Emma Hawksworth, trundling a wheelbarrow.

'Course – things for the homeless!'

The Brownies were having an Effort, collecting household things for the homeless. This pair were evidently worn out. Caroline dropped the handles of the barrow.

'Your turn,' she told Emma.

'Let's look.' Posy started rummaging through. 'Ooh, cushions – what're those? – ooh, knives and forks. And a clock! Ace! Total!'

'Doesn't work.'

'Bet my dad could fix it,' Posy said.

''T'isn't for your dad. It's for the homeless.'

46

'Oh come *on*,' said Emma, taking the handles. 'It's miles yet to the hall – we'll be late for dinner.'

Posy thought fast.

'Tell you what. Leave the barrow at my house, if you like.'

They stared, eyes suspicious, though they could not for the life of them imagine why Posy might have designs on this load of old rubbish.

'Then I could push it up to the hall later.'

'Mind you do!' Emma told her.

'Or you'll have Pearly after you!' warned

Caroline. 'Thanks, Posy. Come on!'

'Oh brilling, oh total!' sang Posy Bates, regarding her barrow full of treasure. 'That'll look nice, that picture of boats. Oh – and curtains!'

They were of faded gold velvet, and would reach right down to the floor in the hen-house, like something out of a magazine.

'Hey – Posy!'

It was Sam, swinging on his gate.

'Was she there? What about my two quid?'

'Oh!' Posy gasped. The poster – the reward!

That poster was still in the window of the Post Office. It was Saturday. Soon half the children in the village would be out combing field and hedgerow. She took to her heels, the barrow abandoned.

'Yes – thanks! Can't stop! See you later!'

She hoped she wasn't too late. She hoped that no one else would find the bag lady holed up in her barn full of straw. For one thing, the old lady might take fright and move off. For another, Posy couldn't afford to dole out more rewards.

'Wouldn't count, anyway,' she comforted herself. 'The reward goes to the first person to find her.'

She even wondered whether Mrs Parkins could be persuaded to refund the twenty pence for putting the poster in the window.

'Hasn't been in there seven hours, let alone seven days,' she thought.

She had reached the post office now, and pushed at the door. It did not budge.

'Whatever . . . ?'

There hung the card. CLOSED. And there hung another notice, with the hours of opening.

'Closed one till two,' she read. 'Oh gubbins!'

That card in the shop door was double bad news. It meant, for one thing, that Posy's reward notice would have to stop in the window for at least another hour, and goodness knew how many people were already combing the village for the bag lady.

'Should've remembered to take it out when I bought the pie,' she thought. 'Oh, double gubbins!'

What the card also meant was that it must be already past one o'clock, and what that meant was that Posy was late for dinner, and what *that* meant was that she'd be in trouble.

'Oh, you do still live here, then?' said Daff, as Posy burst in, hot and breathless, Buggins hard on her heels.

'Sorry, Mum, had to do an errand!'

'What, a Bad Deed for the day?' asked Pippa. She had become increasingly ratty since she went on her diet. She seemed to be eating only lettuce leaves and crispbread.

'Sort of,' said Posy. 'Where's my dinner?'

'It's under the grill,' replied Daff. 'And if there's anything nastier than fried egg left under the grill, I don't know what it is. The yolk'll be all to leather, and serve you right, Posy.'

Posy fetched an oven glove and took the plate out.

'You'll get spotty eating all those chips,' said Pippa jealously.

'You get spotty without them,' Posy told her.

The fried egg looked like a joke one made of plastic, and the baked beans didn't bode well, either. They looked decidedly juiceless. But she reminded herself that to the bag lady, this would be a feast. She splashed it generously with tomato ketchup and began to eat.

A glance at the clock told Posy it was half past one.

'I'll take Fred for a push round after dinner, if you like,' she offered. She meant she'd push him straight round to the shop, where she'd take that WANTED poster out of the window.

'I think I'd lose weight quicker if I had a reward,' said Pippa, eyes fixed on Posy's plate.

'I don't know why you want to lose weight at all,' Daff told her. 'You look all right to me. I don't want you ending up anorexic.'

'Oh Mum, my hips are enormous!'

'Your bottom, you mean,' said Posy.

'You be quiet! But Mum, if I had a reward, something to look forward to . . .'

Posy could read her like an open book. She was going to start on again about having her ears pierced.

'Well, I'm not giving you one,' Daff said.

'I don't mean money. Something like . . . well, like having my ears pierced.'

'Bingo!' Posy Bates told herself.

From here on she knew the dialogue almost by heart. She, for one, would be glad when Pippa did finally get her ears pierced. She wisely decided not to say anything about paint. In her present mood, Daff would veto that as decisively as she was now banning pierced ears.

'Just one of them,' Pippa was begging.

'She might as well ask for a ring through her nose,' Posy thought.

She finished her dinner and went up to get Fred ready for his outing. While she did so, she told him about Sam's trick of saying sorry when you are not really.

'So now you know what to do, if you don't want to tell a fib, a whopper, a porky!'

Fred plucked at his lip with a chubby finger.

'A porky is short for porky pie. It's rhyming slang – porky pie – lie. Get it?'

Fred did not look as if he had got it.

'I'll give you another example. Apples and pears – stairs. See? It rhymes – pears and stairs.'

Fred smiled then, his ravishing slow smile.

'It's what Cockneys do. Though come to think of it, anyone could. I could. Posy Bates' rhyming slang! I'll do one for you. Fred . . . now, what rhymes with that . . . ?'

She pondered as she pulled up his pants.

'I know – bed! Fred, Fred, unmade bed!'

He laughed with her. His laughs were infectious, like measles.

'Now me, Posy . . . cosy . . . dozy . . . I'm definitely not having them. Posy, gozy, hozy, jozy . . .'

She worked her way through the alphabet in search of a suitable rhyme. The best she could come up with was rosy.

'I'm not having panty-hosy,' she told Fred, 'and I'm not having dim and dozy, or anything to do with nosy. So . . . pink and rosy, I suppose. Bit wet . . .'

She carried him down and plonked him in his pram. On their way to the shop, Posy carried on her lecture about rhyming slang.

'Sometime's the rhyme's invisible,' she told him. 'Like *titfer*. That's hat. Tit for tat – hat. Get it?'

There was no way of telling whether he did or not.

'I could invent a whole new rhyming slang,' she told him. 'Then, when you start talking, you and me could use it. It'd be our secret language.'

She made up her mind that that was exactly what she would do. ''S'easy, once you get the hang of it. Double slam – pram. Soft as silk – milk. You can't do it for everything, of course. I mean, what about cornflakes? Or marmalade?'

She was just nicely getting into her stride when she met Miss Perlethorpe.

'Good afternoon, Posy. Is this your Good Deed for the day?'

She indicated the pram. She was evidently wearing her Brown Owl hat, rather than her schoolteacher's.

'Not really,' Posy replied. 'I like doing it.'

'I have just come from the shop. I saw your

notice in the window.'

'Oh gubbins!' said Posy Bates – to herself.

'What exactly is it all about?'

'Just a joke,' said Posy.

' "If seen, do not tell the police",' quoted Miss Perlethorpe. 'Who is this person, Posy?'

'I don't know.' Nor did she, in the sense that she did not know the bag lady's name, or even whether she had one.

'There is apparently a rather strange person about,' continued Miss Perlethorpe. 'A homeless person, I should imagine.'

'Oh really?'

'I know we are collecting for the homeless, Posy, but we should not become involved personally. We shall hand the things over to the Proper Authorities, and they will deal with the matter.'

Posy said nothing. The less she said, the less she could give away.

'Your mother wouldn't want you mixing with strange persons, Posy.' Miss Perlethorpe was still lecturing. Posy often wondered if she did it in her sleep. 'Certainly not with the kind of person who is wanted by the police. Are you listening?'

'Yes.' This was not strictly true. Posy was trying to work out a rhyming slang for Perlethorpe. This was not easy. It fell into the same category as cornflakes and marmalade.

'You must go to the shop and remove that poster this very minute,' Miss Perlethorpe told her.

'Oh yes, I will!' cried Posy. 'I'll go straight there and do it, I promise!'

Miss Perlethorpe looked startled by this sudden apparent surrender. She was not to know that this was exactly what Posy intended to do anyway, for quite different reasons.

'Good girl!'

Miss Perlethorpe leaned over the pram.

'Icky wicky doo! Icky wicky doo! Widdy doo den?'

Posy listened with disgust. It was exactly this sort of ridiculous talk she was trying to counteract. Nobody was going to grow up to be a genius if they had 'diddy widdy doo' and such said to them the whole time.

'Nice for you to have a little brother, Posy.'

'Oh yes! He's mega! Total!'

Miss Perlethorpe looked startled by this heartfelt testimony.

'Yes, well . . . I was thinking more . . . gives you a sense of responsibility.'

'Oh, he does that, all right,' agreed Posy. 'I change his nappy and feed him and everything. Even if there were just him and me on a desert island, I'd be able to look after him.'

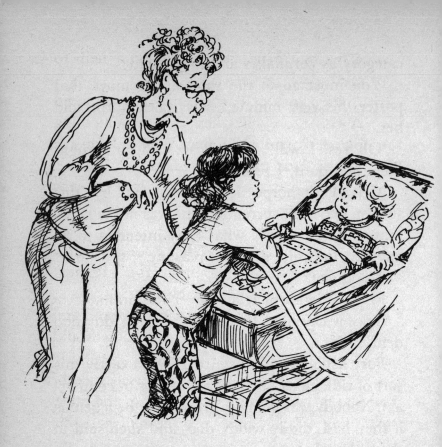

'I should hardly think it will come to that, Posy,' said Miss Perlethorpe.

'You never know,' Posy replied. 'I've thought about it. I'd give him coconut milk, and whenever I found any food, I'd be his tester. You know – like you said kings and popes and that did in the olden days. I'd try the berries or fish and that first, then, if I didn't get belly- I mean, tummy-ache, I'd give them to him.'

This was quite the longest conversation Miss Perlethorpe had ever had with Posy.

'Yes, well, it's nice for you to be a help to your mother,' she said weakly.

'Oh, they aren't Good Deeds,' Posy assured her. 'A Good Deed is when you do something you don't really feel like doing. Why did you say "icky wicky doo" to Fred just now?'

The words were out before she had thought them.

'D-did I?'

'Yes. You said it twice. What does it mean?'

'It – it doesn't mean anything. It's – it's just a way of being pleasant to babies.'

'But if we all said "icky wicky doo" and "diddums" and stuff the whole time, how would babies ever get to talk?'

Miss Perlethorpe was by now herself speechless. She felt quite cornered. Posy, on the other hand, was on firm ground – she had had this conversation many times with Daff.

'Just think, if babies grew up, and all they knew was that stuff, and there were all these grown-ups going round saying "kutchi wutchi coo" and "diddee den" and "icky wicky doo". It'd be terrible, it'd be dire!'

Miss Perlethorpe was stumped, and knew it.

'Yes, well, that's an interesting thought, Posy. Off you go, now, and take that poster down!'

She was off, to do whatever it is that teachers do at weekends.

'Don't think she was listening to a word I said,' Posy told Fred. 'That's the trouble with grown-ups.'

She started to push the pram again.

'Let's see . . . consideration . . . transatlantic . . . and obstreperous! There's three good long words for you!' she told Fred, hoping to cancel out the effects of the 'diddy widdy doos'. 'Now, where were we . . .? Rhyming slang. Perlethorpe's hopeless, so we'll call her Pearly. Here we go . . . burly, curly, early, girly . . . I know! Early! Bright and early! Brighton early . . . it'll be like *titfer*. When I say Brighton it means Brighton early – Pearly! Oh brilling!'

Miss Perlethorpe heard the laughter floating after her, and thought, not for the first time, that Posy Bates really was a mystery.

Five

Posy took the poster from the shop window. She suggested that she might have her money back, as twenty pence was a lot of money to pay for only a few hours. Mrs Parkins did not see it like this. She said it was up to customers when they took their notices down.

'If a lawn mower is sold within the hour, so much the better,' she said. 'A carry cot was once sold when the person who had put up the card was still in the shop. My window is at the very hub of the village.'

Posy did not stop to argue. There was a hen-house to be painted and a bag lady to feed. She bought two bags of crisps and a packet of choc chip cookies.

'Later, I'll make some sandwiches when Mum's not looking,' she told Fred. 'You have a good howl, and while she's seeing to you, I'll do it.'

Fred, however, was already nearly asleep, eye-lids heavy. Posy carried on talking to him regardless. She had heard somewhere that people can hear things when they are asleep, and even learn foreign languages that way.

'I might try it on you,' she told him. 'I could make a tape of some really long words and really interesting information, then play it by your cot at night.'

Usually, Posy would have acted immediately on such an inspiration. This would have to wait.

In the shed she found a brand new tin of white paint. Armed with this and a brush she made for the hen-house.

It was very quiet in there, now that it was henless. The soft slip-slap of the brush on wood was soothing and satisfying.

'I might be a decorator like Dad, when I grow up,' she thought – but not for long. When Posy had swept out earlier on she had only really tackled the floor. It now appeared that the walls were dusty too. (Did hens walk on walls?) The paint was white when it went on. But by the time she had worked it up and down and from side to side, as she had seen George do, something seemed to have happened to it. It became sticky and greyish and full of bits. At the same time, it seemed to disappear, to be sucked into the wood.

This was very disappointing for Posy, who had imagined that to have the interior of the hen-house sparkling white would be short work, a mere doddle. When at last she had finished the first side she stepped back to survey her handiwork. It was, she had to admit, unsatisfactory. It was whit*ish*, but smeary, and the wood was still showing through in places.

'Should've got a proper decorator in,' she thought. 'Dad.'

But George was miles away in his own green cocoon by the river. In any case, though he was usually sympathetic to Posy's ideas, this was rather different.

George might have helped to convert the henhouse into a Wendy house for Posy to play in (not that she would ever have asked for anything so soppy), but even Posy could see that to turn it into a home for a real live bag lady was a bold idea, one probably beyond his grasp.

She laboured on. By the time the second wall was covered, the paint seemed to be getting thicker and thicker, and also decidedly grey.

'Don't have to have all the walls the same colour,' Posy told herself.

She thinned the remaining paint with water from the outside tap, then went into the shed to look for a different colour. There were plenty of tins to choose from, leftovers from George's jobs. The problem was – which to choose?

'Not pink – too wishy washy, and Mum says blue's cold. Yellow I s'pose, or – no – green!

That's it! Then, when she wakes up in the morning, she'll think she's in a field under a hedge, and feel at home!'

The green in question was rather dark. So Posy tipped some of it into the tin of white and gave it a good stir. The resulting shade was not exactly that of a hawthorn hedge, but it was nevertheless green, and as such would be a comfort to the bag lady. Back to the hen-house she trudged, keeping an eye open for Daff.

As Posy was covering the remaining walls with country green, she deliberately did not think of Daff and her possible reaction to a resident bag lady. She thought instead of how the hen-house would soon look with the furnishings she had already collected, the curtains and cane chair, carpet and pictures. She almost began to envy the bag lady.

'It'd suit me,' she thought, 'even if it doesn't suit her.'

That thought was quickly pushed away. There must be no question of it not suiting the bag lady.

'Done!'

Posy laid down her brush with relief. What had started as a soothing slip-slap had ended as an arm-aching toil. Nevertheless, she was pleased with her walls – two whitish, two sort of green.

'Subtle,' she told herself. 'Subtle with a *b*.'

In the shed she put her brush in the jam-jar with the others and surveyed the rolled-up length of carpet propped in one corner.

'No harm in putting that down.'

The carpeting was brand new – or had been a couple of years back when it was put in the shed. It was a piece left over from Posy's own bedroom. Daff said they should keep it, because Posy was bound to ruin her carpet sooner or later, and then there would be some spare. It was green, with swirls in a lighter shade. Posy liked the idea that when she and the bag lady woke up each morning they would both see the very same thing.

The carpet was heavier than she had thought. She could not lift it, so had to drag it, and even that was not easy. It was worth it, though. When she finally got it into the hen-house and rolled it out there was an instant, almost magical feeling of home and comfort.

'Even houses don't feel like home with no carpet,' she thought.

She pulled it this way and that, trampling it with her feet to settle it down. It still looked a little like a sea with waves, and Posy walked here and there over it, her steps almost soundless.

'It's eaten all the echoes!' she thought. Then, 'If there were carpets under railway bridges,

perhaps even *they* wouldn't have echoes.'

Under railway bridges was where Posy imagined the bag lady spending many of her nights. There was one thing that particularly worried Posy about this, but each time it floated into her mind she pushed it away. She pushed it away now.

She was so delighted by the sudden comfort of the hen-house that she wanted to go on now, and add the chair, the pictures and the curtains (though these, she realized, would be tricky).

But the picture of her bag lady, hunched in that shadowy barn kept floating into her mind.

Posy could almost hear her belly rumbling.

'Sandwiches!' she thought.

It was just her luck that when she entered the kitchen, Pippa was there. She was looking in the fridge, and jumped back guiltily.

'Just looking,' she said.

The trouble was, she had a slab of pork pie in her hand.

'Put that back!' ordered Posy, thinking how the bag lady would love it. 'Put it back this minute!'

'I was just going to!' and Pippa put it back. 'I was really looking for some lettuce.'

'Pork pie is just about the most fattening thing in the whole world,' Posy told her. 'If you eat that, you'll end up with the most enormous bottom in the whole world. Hips, I mean.'

'I know,' said Pippa miserably. 'But I'm ravenous!'

'Is your belly rumbling?' enquired Posy sympathetically.

'It is, as a matter of fact. And don't be so revolting.'

'Eat an apple. Or an orange. Or a handful of raisins. Or a stick of celery.'

Posy had once been stuck in the dentist's waiting room with nothing but women's magazines to read. She knew a lot about diets, and a lot about not being able to have babies.

Pippa was already scrunching an apple.

'When you've had it, have a good run round,' Posy advised. 'You've got to diet *and* exercise!'

She was really quite uninterested in Pippa's bottom. But she wanted her out of the way, while she scavenged things for the bag lady.

'It's all right for you. You're skinny however much you eat,' Pippa said. 'It's disgusting. It's not fair.'

'Life *isn't* fair,' replied Posy. 'It ought to be, but it's not.'

She knew this for a fact. It was something she thought about practically every day of her life. It wasn't fair that Sam had beautiful golden hair and her own was mousey. It wasn't fair that millions of people all over the world were starving. Or that Miss Perlethorpe thought Mary Pye was a good, helpful girl, when in fact she was a rat. Or that there were homeless people who had to roam the wide world in all weathers and sleep under hedges.

The minute Pippa went out, Posy took the pork pie from the fridge and put it in a bag. She found some sliced bread and smeared it hastily with peanut butter. She added a tomato.

'For vitamins,' she thought. 'Bet she doesn't get many vitamins. Wonder if she knows about there being vitamins in stinging nettles?'

She took a half full bottle of lemonade. It would take too long to make tea, and Daff might appear at any moment.

'In any case, I don't know if she likes milk and sugar, or sweeteners.'

There were a lot of things she did not know about the bag lady. That was half her charm.

'I don't even know her *name*!'

Posy was not sure that she wanted to. Perhaps if Posy knew her name, her mysteriousness would vanish.

'It would if it was Ethel. Or Glenys. Or

Mavis. Ethel Smith. Glenys Williams. Mavis Jones.'

None of them sounded remotely right. Posy decided then and there never to ask the bag lady her name.

'If her mother was a rotten name-picker, like mine, it could be anything!'

Being Posy, she then started wondering what the bag lady's mother could possibly have been like, or even if she had ever had one.

She put the picnic in her rucksack, called, 'Shan't be long!' to anyone who might be listening, and set off for the barn.

She could not be absolutely certain that the bag lady would still be there. She had made no promises. Now that she had her precious picture of the cat, she might have taken off again, up hill, down dale.

'If she is still there, wonder what she's been doing all afternoon?'

Not knitting, not doing crossword puzzles, not doing her washing and ironing. What, then?

'Must have some books in those bags,' Posy decided. '*Must* have. How'd she ever manage without?'

She herself could not, she knew that for a fact. A world without books was unthinkable.

The bag lady was neither knitting nor doing crossword puzzles nor reading. She had her eyes shut. Posy paused for a moment in the doorway, just taking in that already familiar figure. It was as good a chance as she would ever have to look at her, *really* look. You couldn't do that when people were awake – it was called staring, and was rude.

That face under the frizzed hair and grubby hat was as calm and peaceful as a baby's. Even Fred could not look more blissfully out of this world. It occurred to Posy that perhaps the bag lady's happiest times were spent sleeping – or at any rate, with her eyes shut, daydreaming. She wondered what dreams the bag lady had, and hoped that they included ones of snug hen-houses with carpets and cushions.

'Deserves to have a dream come true,' she thought. 'We *all* do, but specially her.'

She coughed delicately. The bag lady must

have been daydreaming because next moment her eyes were wide open and looking into Posy's own.

'I've brought some stuff,' Posy said. 'Pork pie and biscuits and that.'

She went from the sunlight into the shadows, took off her rucksack and began to unpack it.

'Hope you like peanut butter – couldn't find anything else except jam, and that's bad for your teeth.'

Whether the bag lady did or did not, she certainly wolfed those sandwiches down.

'She's *always* hungry!' thought Posy. 'It's not that long since she had that pie!'

On the other hand, if you never knew where the next meal was coming from, or even whether there would be a meal at all, perhaps you ate whenever you had the chance. (Posy had the feeling that camels did this, too.) Down went the pie, the sandwiches, the tomato. Posy didn't like to interrupt her when she was so furiously busy eating, but knew she could not stop for long. She had already upset her mother once today, by being late for dinner. Daff had to be kept in a good mood if she was soon to be presented with a bag lady.

'You'll stop tonight, won't you?' she asked anxiously.

There was no reply, one way or the other.

'I've got to go now, but I can bring some more food tomorrow. And listen, I've got a lovely surprise for you! And I can show it you tomorrow, even if it's not quite ready. You'll like it, honestly you will!'

The old lady munched and stared, munched and stared. It was impossible to tell what she was thinking. Posy felt quite desperate. Somehow or other she had to make it plain that if the bag lady moved on tonight she would miss the biggest and best surprise of her whole life.

'It's a reward!' she said, with sudden inspiration – and so it was, a much better reward than two pounds, or pierced ears. 'If you're still here tomorrow, there'll be a reward!'

She ran then, to put the finishing touches to that reward, and leaving the bag lady to finish her lonely feast in the hay.

Six

There was still much to be done.

'But the worst's over,' Posy told herself. 'Painting was the worst.'

Now came the enjoyable part, the furnishing of the hen-house, the little finishing touches that would make it a real home.

It was just her luck, she thought, that on her way home she should meet Miss Perlethorpe. It was even worse luck that Miss Perlethorpe had heard about the barrowload of things for the homeless collected by Caroline Boot and Emma Hawksworth.

'They told me you said you would wheel it up to the hall,' she said severely. 'A Brownie keeps her promises, Posy Bates.'

'The minute I've had tea,' said Posy – out loud. Inside her head she added 'Once I've helped myself to a few things off it.'

She had no qualms about this. The things were for the homeless, and the bag lady was certainly that. Posy took the gold velvet curtains, the picture of boats, a few knives and forks and the clock. It wasn't working, but perhaps it soon would be. A companionably ticking clock would certainly make any hen-house seem like home. She shook it a few times, hopefully, but it remained stubbornly dumb. She did find a yellow teapot, though, and a mixture of plates, and added them to her pile. She had never, of course, seen the bag lady eat off a plate, with a knife and fork, but supposed she must remember how.

'Must've done, once,' she thought. 'Her mum'd never've let her eat like that.'

Daff certainly would not.

Then she found the bookends, in the shape of dolphins.

'Oh ace, oh total!' she sang, and could see in her mind's eye the bag lady sitting in the cane chair, lost in a book while rain pattered on the roof and ran down the little windows. It was a picture of heaven.

The beautiful yellow Saturday hours were ticking by, fast as never before. By the time Posy had had tea and trundled the barrow up to the village hall, then returned the barrow to Emma's house, the light was fading. There was barely time to carry a few cushions and a toasting fork to the hen-house.

'Get up early in the morning and finish it,' Posy decided. 'Set my alarm.'

Before going to bed she looked in on Fred.

'I ought to have prepared him, like I did with Buggins,' she thought. 'Else he might get a shock, and howl.'

Fred was fast asleep, his tiny fists curled. Now was the time for Posy to test the theory that people hear things even when they are asleep.

'I'll make it into a kind of story,' she decided. 'Make it more interesting for him.'

So she settled herself by his cot, and softly told him the story of a bag lady who wandered the wide world. She slept under hedges and was woken, with dew in her boots, by the crowing of cocks. She slept under bridges, and all night long the trains rumbled and echoed through her sleep. Wherever she went, people stared, or turned their eyes away, pretending she was not there. Children laughed at her, policemen moved her on. And all the while, or nearly all the while, her belly was rumbling with hunger. She explained that the bag lady was rather dirty and smelly, she could not help being so. She even confided the secret worry she had, the one she kept pushing away whenever it came into her mind.

'And listen, I don't even know where she goes to the lav, but she must do – everybody does.'

As an afterthought, she added, 'Not that you know about that, yet. But *she* hasn't got a nappy, and someone to change it.'

She felt better now that she had shared this worry, even if only with the gently breathing Fred.

'So tomorrow you'll meet her,' she finished, and her heart beat faster at the thought. 'And I want you to give a really big smile, like the ones you give me. She'll like that. I don't think she gets smiled at much.'

She got to her feet and looked down at Fred and wondered if her story was already printed in his head and whether, when he remembered it, it would seem as if he had always known it.

'I'll find out, the minute he starts to talk,' she thought. 'To knife and fork – talk.'

She awoke at exactly seven o'clock and swiftly stopped the alarm. Not that there was much danger of anyone else being roused at this time on a Sunday, and Pippa could sleep through the alarm even when it was right next to her bed.

As she quietly opened the back door and stepped outside, Posy was glad she had the world to herself. And when she went into the hen-house she saw how beautifully lit it was by the early sun, and how the shadows of apple trees danced on the green and whitish walls.

'It's happening,' she thought, half awed, 'it *is* turning into a home!'

The carpet was still ever-so-slightly wavy, so she gave it another trample before fetching the cane chair.

'Now the table!'

Posy did not have a table, as such, but was not deterred. She had picked up a useful furnishing hint from Pippa (who in turn had picked it up from a magazine). She draped empty boxes with pieces of lace or patchwork, and used them as tables. Posy draped her box with a curtain, cream with poppies. She found a hammer and nails and put up her pictures – one of boats, the other of a ruined church or abbey. There was an armful of cushions, assorted shapes, sizes and colours like Liquorice Allsorts. These she arranged in little inviting heaps.

'For visitors,' she thought – meaning herself, mainly.

The dolphin bookends, she decided, must go on the floor for the time being. And because they looked rather as though they did not know what they were doing, or why they were there, she fetched some books to put between them. She had no idea what the bag lady's taste in reading was, so brought a selection. There were some of her own favourites – *The Hobbit* and *Five Children and It* – a few of Daff's paperbacks and a book called *Birds of the British Isles* in case the bag lady decided to take up bird watching. She would be living, after all, in a kind of hide.

Posy supposed that the bag lady would sleep on the floor, but at least that, unlike the bottom of a hedge or under a railway bridge, was carpeted. She neatly folded three blankets and covered them with the other poppy curtain.

'Nearly ready!'

There were only the finishing touches now. A decorated tin for a store of biscuits, the brass

toasting fork hung on a nail, a jug of marigolds
on the table.

'There!' She stepped back and admired her
handiwork and it was so much better than she
had even dreamed that she could barely breathe
for pride and excitement. She wanted to run off
now, this very moment, to fetch the bag lady
from her shadowy barn and show her, and see
those fierce, suspicious eyes light up.

But first she must go through the usual
Sunday morning motions, she knew that. And
so she did. She went in and had breakfast and
was amazed that she was able to behave in such

an ordinary, everyday way, when she was hugging such a thrilling secret.

'Could be an actress,' she told herself (though this would be a long way down her list of possible careers).

Posy had decided early on that it would not be a good idea to prepare Daff for the bag lady's arrival. If she did that, there would be no arrival to prepare *for*. She must establish the bag lady in her hen-house, then tell. It would be much harder, she argued, to turn somebody out than to prevent her coming in the first place.

Mum might even *like* her,' she thought, but not with any real conviction. Daff, like Miss Perlethorpe, probably preferred the homeless at a safe distance.

'. . . so it'll just be something cold today,' she heard Daff say. 'Are you listening, Posy? And just because it's cold there's no need to think you can be late for it.'

'Sorry – what?'

'Your father's going to give the kitchen a lick of paint,' said Daff. 'You'll find a new tin, George, in the shed.'

Posy thought she could actually feel herself turning pale. There was no new tin in the shed, she knew that. What little was left in that tin was not even white any more. It was hedge-bottom green.

There was never going to be a good day to introduce the bag lady into the Bates household, Posy knew that, had known it all along. But today, once Daff discovered what had happened to the paint, was going to be the worst possible.

'Too late, though,' Posy thought. '*Got* to bring her today. Might be my only chance ever.'

She wished now she had painted those walls orange, black, violet, sky blue, pink with spots on – anything but that white meant for the kitchen. One thing was certain – she had to make her escape to the barn before Daff discovered what had happened.

'Stay, Buggins!' she ordered, as she stuffed some crisps into the bag containing the two slices of toast she had managed to palm at breakfast. 'I'm off to fetch somebody – a stray, like you.'

As Posy hurried through the village she willed the bag lady to be still in the barn. She willed so hard that her teeth gritted and her hands clenched. She felt clenched all over.

As she approached Potters' barn she went slower and slower. If the bag lady had vanished, she did not want to know. She stopped outside the leaning, ramshackle door. She held her breath and shut her eyes.

'Twice round the garden shed, once round the sundial, clap your hands five times, shut your eyes and say the magic word!'

She waited a moment to give the spell time to work, opened her eyes and pushed the door.

'There!'

And so she was, exactly the same as ever, except for wisps of straw sticking to her hair and clothes. Posy could have hugged her.

Instead, she offered the bag containing food.

'There's not much, I'm afraid,' she said, 'but there'll be lots more later.'

The bag lady set to demolishing the toast first, in great hungry bites.

'Tell her now,' thought Posy, and wished she had rehearsed exactly what she would say. As it was, the words came tumbling out all anyhow.

'When you've finished I've got something to show you – a surprise – the reward I told you about yesterday!'

Champ champ. Crunch crunch.

'It's at my house – not exactly at my house – in the garden, and it's for you. I did it specially and I think it might be your dream come true!'

The old lady certainly seemed to be listening. As she crunched she was watching Posy, head cocked, like a bird.

'I can't tell you much more, it'd give it away and then it wouldn't be a surprise, but I'll give you a clue! You might never have to sleep under a bridge again – never!'

The bag lady absently wiped her mouth with

her grubby sleeve.

'And I'd bring you food every day,' added Posy cunningly. 'So will you come and look? Will you?'

To her astonishment the bag lady nodded, got to her feet and matter-of-factly picked up her bags. She looked as unconcerned as a passenger whose train has just drawn in.

'I'll carry one – let me!' Posy reached for one of the bulging bags. She looked sideways up at that weather-beaten face and felt shy, almost, and for the first time a little fearful that perhaps the bag lady would not like the hen-house, would be disappointed by it.

The pair of them left the barn and followed the narrow lane up to the village. As they went, the bells started to ring from the church. Posy groaned.

'Should've *thought*! Should've waited till they were all in church!'

It was too late now. She and the bag lady would have to meet the people flocking in their Sunday best – the old ladies with their flowery hats, children in neat white socks, possibly Pearly in her pearls.

They emerged from the lane and on to the green, the bag lady huffing and puffing now, Posy with her chin defiantly in the air. It was only when she saw Pearly, in her dark blue, and

behind her the little string of brown-clad figures,
that she remembered.

The special service for the homeless! The
Brownies were carrying offerings, as they did
at Harvest Festival. Only today they were not
potatoes or vegetable marrows, they were table
lamps, cushions, teapots, blankets. Even that
hateful Mary Pye was carrying a scrubbing
brush.

Posy tried to hang back, but the bag lady kept
on, blithely unaware that she was one of the
Homeless with a capital H. Miss Perlethorpe
was bound to spot her – and did.

'Wait!' Posy heard her say, and then she was
pounding over the green crying, 'Posy – Posy

Bates! Why aren't you in your uniform – and where's your offering?' She did not actually say 'And who is this disgusting person?' but she might as well have. The expression on her face said it all.

'Sorry, Miss Perlethorpe,' Posy said, adding to herself, 'I don't think!'

The bag lady kept going. She, after all, was not in Miss Perlethorpe's class, or pack.

'Who's that?' hissed Miss Perlethorpe.

'Just a friend,' said Posy. 'Just a friend I'm helping with her luggage.'

The bells tumbled to a standstill.

'Oh – I'll have to – oh!' and Miss Perlethorpe was off, waving her Brownies furiously towards the church door, postponing the impossible Posy Bates to a later date.

Having faced Miss Perlethorpe, Posy felt curiously light and free, prepared to face the whole world now, let alone a paintless Daff. She caught up with the steadily trudging bag lady.

'Take no notice of her,' she said – unnecessarily. The bag lady had taken no more notice of Miss Perlethorpe than if she had been a buzzing fly – less, probably.

When they reached the garden gate there was no sign of Daff or George, no sign of anyone. Posy fixed her eyes on the hen-house in its orchard.

'Nearly there,' she said encouragingly. She pushed open the gate, hardly able to believe that she was playing hostess to this exotic creature. Nothing else in the world mattered. She did not even think of checking that the coast was clear, or wonder what Daff would do if she happened to be looking.

Over the grass they went, under the apple boughs and right to the very door of the hen-house. Posy halted and drew another deep breath. This was it – this was the moment she had dreamed of, and hoped the bag lady had, too. She flung open the door.

'There!'

The bag lady looked. She saw the wavy carpet, the cane chair, cushions, marigolds. Posy had a sudden irreverent thought that perhaps she should have baited the hen-house, like a mousetrap. She should have placed a large slice of pork pie, or hunk of cake on the table.

Then the bag lady put down her bags. Then she put her head right inside and peered about. And then she went in! She went straight to the cane chair and sat in it, wedged in very tightly because of her bulging layers of clothes. To Posy, she looked like a queen on her throne.

'Do – do you like it?' Her voice came out as a croak.

The bag lady heaved a sigh and stuck her legs out straight and folded her arms.

'Oh, icky comfy, icky nice!'

She was saying it to herself, Posy knew that, and as she watched, the merest hint of a smile flickered over the bag lady's face. And then she closed her eyes.

The bag lady had come home.

Other great reads ✏ *from* **Red Fox**

Further Red Fox titles that you might enjoy reading are listed on the following pages. They are available in bookshops or they can be ordered directly from us.

If you would like to order books, please send this form and the money due to:

ARROW BOOKS, BOOKSERVICE BY POST, PO BOX 29, DOUGLAS, ISLE OF MAN, BRITISH ISLES. Please enclose a cheque or postal order made out to Arrow Books Ltd for the amount due, plus 75p per book for postage and packing to a maximum of £7.50, both for orders within the UK. For customers outside the UK, please allow £1.00 per book.

NAME_____

ADDRESS_____

_____

Please print clearly.

Whilst every effort is made to keep prices low, it is sometimes necessary to increase cover prices at short notice. If you are ordering books by post, to save delay it is advisable to phone to confirm the correct price. The number to ring is THE SALES DEPARTMENT 071 (if outside London) 973 9700.

Other great reads *from* **Red Fox**

Have a bundle of fun with the wonderful Pat Hutchins

Pat Hutchins' stories are full of wild adventure and packed with outrageous humour for younger readers to enjoy.

FOLLOW THAT BUS

A school party visit to a farm ends in chaotic comedy when two robbers steal the school bus.

ISBN 0 09 993220 2   £2.99

THE HOUSE THAT SAILED AWAY

An hilarious story of a family afloat, in their house, in the Pacific Ocean. No matter what adventures arrive, Gran always has a way to deal with them.

ISBN 0 09 993200 8   £2.99

RATS!

Sam's ploys to persuade his parents to let him have a pet rat eventually meet with success, and with Nibbles in the house, life is never the same again.

ISBN 0 09 993190 7   £2.50